# If I had a pig
## MICK INKPEN

WITH CARE

# M
MACMILLAN CHILDREN'S BOOKS

First published in Great Britain 1988 by
MACMILLAN CHILDREN'S BOOKS
A division of Macmillan Publishers Limited
London and Basingstoke
Associated companies throughout the world

Reprinted 1989

British Library Cataloguing in Publication Data
Inkpen, Mick
If I had a pig.
I. Title
823'.914[J]      PZ7

ISBN 0-333-44863-4

Printed in Hong Kong

If I had a pig...

I would tell him...

...a joke.

I would hide from him…

...and jump out. Boo!

We could make a house...

...and have our friends to stay.

We could paint pictures...

...of each other.

We could have fights...

...and piggybacks.

On his birthday...

...I would bake him a cake.

I would race him...

...to the park.

If it snowed...

We could stay in the bath...

...if it rained.

...I would make him a snowpig.

We would need our boots...

...until we wrinkled up.

I would read him a story...

...and take him to bed.